HIP-HOP ARTISTS

KID CUDI

RAPPER AND RECORD EXECUTIVE

BY JILL C. WHEELER

Essential Library
An Imprint of Abdo Publishing
abdobooks.com

ABDOBOOKS.COM

Published by Abdo Publishing, a division of ABDO, PO Box 398166, Minneapolis, Minnesota 55439.

Printed in the United States of America, North Mankato, Minnesota.
102021
012022

Cover Photo: Zach Cordner/Invision/AP/Shutterstock Images
Interior Photo: Phillip Faraone/Getty Images Entertainment/Getty Images, 4, 8; Kathy Hutchins/Shutterstock Images, 11, 76; Shutterstock Images, 12, 22, 26–27, 91; Joe Seer/Shutterstock Images, 15; Tony Dejak/AP Images, 16; Pedro Gutierrez/Shutterstock Images, 19; Randy Miramontez/Shutterstock Images, 21; Debby Wong/Shutterstock Images, 25; Johnny Nunez/WireImage/Getty Images, 28; Alex J. Berliner/abimages/AP Images, 30–31; Jim Cooper/AP Images, 35; Nejron Photo/Shutterstock Images, 38; AD1/Wenn/Newscom, 41; Kyle Gustafson/Zuma Press/Alamy, 43; AF Archive/Alamy, 45, 60, 65; Jake Coyle/AP Images, 48; Lionel Hahn/Abaca Press/Alamy, 53; Scott Roth/Invision/AP Images, 56; Steve C. Mitchell/Invision/AP Images, 62–63; Moviestore Collection Ltd/Alamy, 66–67, 83; Willy Sanjuan/Invision/AP Images, 68; Timothy Norris/Getty Images for Coachella/Getty Images Entertainment/Getty Images, 72–73; Ovidiu Hrubaru/Shutterstock Images, 74; Christian Bertrand/Shutterstock Images, 78; Yui Mok/PA Wire/AP Images, 81; Daniel DeSlover/Sipa USA/AP Images, 84; Kit Lau/Shutterstock Images, 86; Amy Harris/Invision/AP Images, 88–89; Laurent Vu/Sipa/AP Images, 93; Featureflash Photo Agency/Shutterstock Images, 95; Miguel Vasconcellos/Zuma Press/Newscom, 96

Editor: Arnold Ringstad
Series Designer: Laura Graphenteen

LIBRARY OF CONGRESS CONTROL NUMBER: 2021941086

PUBLISHER'S CATALOGING-IN-PUBLICATION DATA

Names: Wheeler, Jill C., author.
Title: Kid Cudi: rapper and record executive / by Jill C. Wheeler
Other title: rapper and record executive
Description: Minneapolis, Minnesota : Abdo Publishing, 2022 | Series: Hip-hop artists | Includes online resources and index.
Identifiers: ISBN 9781532196164 (lib. bdg.) | ISBN 9781098217976 (ebook)
Subjects: LCSH: Kid Cudi (Scott Mescudi), 1984---Juvenile literature. | Rap musicians --United States--Biography--Juvenile literature. | Rap (Music)--Juvenile literature. | Lyricists--Biography--Juvenile literature. | Actors--Biography--Juvenile literature.
Classification: DDC 782.421649--dc23

CONTENTS

Chapter ONE

ONE COURAGEOUS VOICE

November 5, 2016, marked the opening of the first-ever ComplexCon event, an entertainment festival showcasing pop culture, street style, hip-hop, and more. Fans began lining up at the convention center in Long Beach, California, before the doors opened, and some 10,000 attendees streamed in when the event began.[1] Inside, they found displays of the latest sneaker styles and streetwear, food booths, celebrities, panel discussions, and best of all, stages for musical performances.

Much of the buzz that day centered on the evening's featured musical acts. Kid Cudi was on the bill, along with Travis Scott and headliner Skrillex. For fans of Kid Cudi in particular, it would be a very special gig.

Kid Cudi's performance at ComplexCon in 2016 marked his return to the music world, and fans were not disappointed.

Just one month earlier, Cudi had surprised his fans and the music world with an announcement on his Facebook page. He said he was taking a break from performing to get treatment for depression and suicidal thoughts. "My anxiety and depression have ruled my life for as long as I can remember," he wrote in his post. "I can't make new friends because of it. I don't trust anyone because of it and I'm tired of being held back in my life."[2]

Cudi's post was unusual within the hip-hop world, where masculinity had historically been emphasized at the expense of heartfelt feelings and emotions. Artists who violated that norm were considered soft or weak and usually faced a negative backlash. Yet Cudi had never shied away from talking about how he was feeling.

DEPRESSION

The American Psychiatric Association (APA) describes depression as a common and serious medical illness. Depression affects how a person feels, how a person thinks, and how a person acts, all in negative ways. Common symptoms that might indicate depression include feeling sad often and losing interest in doing things that used to be enjoyable.

It is estimated that about one in every 15 adults suffers from depression in any given year. Fortunately, depression can be treated successfully with methods including medications and talk therapy. The APA estimates that between 80 and 90 percent of people with depression get better over time with treatment.[3]

Cudi's songs addressed difficult emotions, including loneliness, loss, and grief.

Cudi found his fans to be supportive of his decision to enter treatment. His post received a flood of positive replies. In return, Cudi assured his fans that he would be back. And on November 5, he kept his promise. The Grammy winner and fashion icon appeared on the ComplexCon stage wearing jeans, a jacket, and a simple white Henley shirt. The crowd was already pumped following an energetic performance by Cudi's friend and mentee, Travis Scott. At Cudi's appearance, the audience members broke into applause for a full 30 seconds. "Feels good to be free," he told them.[4]

RAP, HIP-HOP, AND HYPERMASCULINITY

Rap and hip-hop have been called out for their focus on hypermasculinity. This is exaggerated, stereotypical male behavior, including an emphasis on physical strength, aggression, and male sexuality. *Hip-Hop: Beyond Beats and Rhymes*, a film by award-winning documentary filmmaker Byron Hurt, explores the roots of this focus.

The film examines how racism, poverty, and violence have contributed to a culture where being weak can get you killed. Scholar Jelani Cobb explains in the film that boasting and swagger are central to the history of hip-hop because of the trauma in the history of Black men in America. "There's a whole lineage of Black men wanting to deny their own frailty," Cobb says. "In some ways you have to do that . . . like a psychic armor."[5]

Just as Cudi's fans were thrilled to see him return to the stage, he was glad to be back.

Cudi then launched into a set of fan favorites, including "Pursuit of Happiness," "Erase Me," and "Frequency." He addressed the crowd during a break: "Listen, I miss every single one of you," he said. "I know life is crazy . . . but we can make it through. I am living proof."[6]

INFLUENCING THE INFLUENCERS

Few performers have had as much impact on their industries as Kid Cudi. Cudi, whose real name is Scott Mescudi (pronounced MESS-kud-ee), burst upon the scene in 2008 with hooks that captured the attention of rap superstar Kanye West. Cudi quickly moved from singer and songwriter to producer, constantly experimenting with combinations of genres. He mixed conventional hip-hop, alternative rock, jazz, soul, pop, and more. He later expanded his career with successful ventures in acting and directing music videos. His eye for style and design has earned him a host of fashion-conscious

THE PURSUIT OF "PURSUIT"

"Pursuit of Happiness" is Kid Cudi's most successful song to date, having been certified platinum multiple times over. The song began with a beat that Evan Mast of the electronic rock group Ratatat created on a synthesizer keyboard. Mast then combined it with a progression of piano chords, all while Cudi was driving over to Mast's house.

"He's . . . literally in a car on his way over and I'm feeling around the keyboard," Mast recalls. "I had a sound that I created on that keyboard, and I was like, 'Well maybe I can do something with this?' Basically as fast as possible, [I] just laid that down and then the doorbell rings. . . . Instantly, [Kid Cudi] heard that beat and he was like, 'Oh, yeah.'"[7]

followers as well as licensing deals from clothing and shoe companies.

Perhaps most dramatically, Cudi has paved the way for a new generation of artists to address the emotional challenges of life. His first hit, 2008's "Day 'N' Nite," reflected the loneliness and pain he felt at the loss of a relative with whom he had an unresolved conflict. His first album, 2009's *Man on the Moon: The End of Day*, blended a spectrum of raw emotions, including anxiety, sadness, and unbridled joy.

Cudi is credited with helping expand the range of topics hip-hop artists could address with their music. Hip-hop artist and producer Evan Mast of electronic rock duo Ratatat said Cudi's use of emotion and vulnerabilities initially created a shock to the hip-hop system. "To have somebody get on the microphone and express these vulnerabilities was

RATATAT

Frequent Kid Cudi collaborator Ratatat is a Brooklyn-based electronic rock duo. The band, made up of Mike Stroud and Evan Mast, focuses on instrumental music in the hip-hop, electronic, and rock genres. The two artists met while students at Skidmore College. Ratatat records songs without lyrics, which the duo says enables listeners to add their own mental pictures of what the songs might be about. The two typically begin with a beat, over which they layer keyboards and guitars.

Cudi has become known for his creativity and originality in the worlds of both music and fashion.

definitely not something you were used to hearing at that time," he said.[8]

Fellow artists are quick to note that part of Cudi's influence is due to his confidence. "Cudi . . . represents the freedom to be into many things," says singer-songwriter Pharrell Williams. "[He can] have a really serious, informed opinion about those things to take what he likes in terms of inspiration and be able to turn it into a solid thought or concept. . . . He also marches to the beat of his own drum."[9]

Stars such as Pharrell Williams have praised Cudi's confidence and craft.

SLOW AND STEADY BURN

Critics acknowledge that Cudi's confidence is part of the reason he has been able to change what is acceptable in hip-hop. The fresh sounds, energy, and attitude that marked his work in the late 2000s decade have continued to lead the way in hip-hop's exciting evolution. Cudi's first success, "Day 'N' Nite," reached Number 3 on the *Billboard* Hot 100 in May 2009. Eleven years later, in May 2020, Cudi's "The Scotts" debuted at Number 1 on the same chart. "The Scotts" is a collaboration with Travis Scott, who based his stage name on Cudi's given name due to Cudi's influence on his work.

Cudi released the first album in his *Man on the Moon* trilogy in September 2009. The critically acclaimed album sold more than 100,000 copies in its first week.[10] In November 2010, Cudi released the second album in the series, which debuted at Number 4 on the *Billboard* 200. December 2020 saw the release of the third and final *Man on the Moon* effort. It quickly reached Number 1 on *Billboard*'s Top R&B/Hip-Hop Albums chart.

In 2016, Cudi's original mentor and longtime collaborator, Kanye West, referred to Cudi as the "most influential artist of the past ten years."[11] In addition to

Cudi has been recognized by the Grammys and other awards organizations during his career.

West, many other fellow hip-hop artists have praised Cudi, including Logic, Kyle, and Jaden Smith. Travis Scott has said, "I would [tour with Cudi] for free. . . . He's probably one of the realest rappers alive."[12]

Cudi has had four Grammy nominations and one Grammy win over the years, as well as a host of other honors and recognitions. Yet these formal awards fail to acknowledge the full impact Cudi has had on his fans. *Saturday Night Live* star Pete Davidson, who has suffered from depression, literally credited Cudi for saving his life. "If you're 25 and under, I truly believe that Kid Cudi saved your life," he said in a 2016 interview.[13] Cudi's contributions to mental health awareness and advocacy were even recognized in a psychology textbook.

Cudi acknowledges that for him, emotions and music are virtually inseparable. "I turn my pain into music," he says. "And my music is how I am different. And my difference is my power."[14]

AMMY® AW
RAM

THE KID FROM CLEVELAND

Chapter Two

Kid Cudi was born Scott Ramon Seguro Mescudi on January 30, 1984, in Cleveland, Ohio. Scott was the youngest of four children born to Lindberg and Elsie (Banks) Mescudi. Lindberg was of Mexican and Native American heritage. A veteran of World War II (1939–1945), Lindberg worked as a housepainter and was also a substitute teacher. Elsie was of African American heritage. She was a classically trained singer and a choir teacher at Roxboro Middle School in Cleveland Heights, Ohio. Scott grew up with two older brothers, Domingo and Dean, and an older sister, Maisha. The family lived in the diverse, mostly well-to-do suburb of Shaker Heights.

Tragedy struck the Mescudi family in 1995 when Lindberg died of cancer. Scott was just 11 years old. "Lin was always a strong force in their lives, and when he got sick, they went through that sickness with him," said Elsie

Cudi returned to his hometown in 2012 for a show organized by the Rock & Roll Hall of Fame.

LOSS OF A PARENT

Losing a parent is one of the most traumatic things that can occur during childhood. Children rely on their parents for safety, security, and certainty, so losing a parent may create fear and uncertainty within children that these important needs will not be met. In addition, losing a parent can create more economic stresses on a family.

Research indicates children who lose a parent are at a higher risk for various negative outcomes. These outcomes may include changes in behavior and increases in sleep disturbances. In addition, children who have lost a parent are at greater risk for anxiety, depression, reduced academic success, and lower self-esteem.

Mescudi about her children. "They were there every day after school, even when it got real bad. So it was a devastating time for all of them—Scott especially, because he was the baby. There's a sadness [in him] because of the void."[1]

The loss left Scott struggling with dreams of dying in a bus or car accident. He remembers sleeping with his mother on the family couch until he was 12 due to his nightmares. "She'd get so [upset] when I did it, but I'd be like, 'I can't sleep!'" he recalls.[2] His mother quickly realized her youngest son had artistic talents, however, and she encouraged him to pursue those interests. She pushed him to join the choir at Roxboro Middle School, and it was there that he received his first standing ovation.

Cudi grew up in the Cleveland, Ohio, area.

It came after a performance of R. Kelly's "I Believe I Can Fly" in a school choir concert.

Roxboro also was where Scott found a mentor, art teacher Keaf Holliday. At that time, Scott was into art and enjoyed drawing, including designing tattoos. Holliday recalls that even as a middle school student, Scott had a sense of style. "The very first time I met Scott, he was wearing this real sharp black outfit," Holliday recalls. "I was doing some pastel

"I was in the kitchen, cleaning, when I heard this voice. I was like, 'Whoa!' He has an absolutely gorgeous voice."[3]

—Elsie Mescudi on hearing Scott sing at home

drawing. I said, 'Hey, Scott, do you want to try some of this?' He said, 'Man, I don't want to get my clothes dirty.'"[4]

LIL SCOTT

In addition to singing, Scott attempted to learn the trumpet, the clarinet, and the violin. He says he failed at all of them and eventually realized he did better when playing by ear instead of using sheet music. In school, he struggled to overcome the sadness that had descended upon him following the death of his father. The sadness contributed to his poor grades.

Scott recalls starting to rap with friends from his neighborhood around the age of 12. At that time, he was listening to Lil Wayne and even began calling himself Lil Scott. Later, he shortened his surname and found the stage name that would see him to stardom. While many of his friends lost interest in rapping, Scott did not. He spent hours in his bedroom scribbling lyrics in a notebook and making recordings on karaoke machines and boom boxes. Around the age of 15, his interest in drawing began to take a back seat to his interest in music.

Scott began performing in open mic and freestyle rap competitions. He recalls that Cleveland's hip-hop scene was centered on clubs on the city's west side. He had

As a kid, Scott was a fan of rapper Lil Wayne, whose career began in the late 1990s.

to catch a ride from someone to get there, but it did not stop him from entering the freestyle battles. Some competitions featured a selection of original recordings, and audiences got to vote on their favorites. Whoever won could come back the following week and perform live. "That was my goal," he recalled. "I gotta have this dope song, then I gotta go perform."[5]

The Wu-Tang Clan was among Scott's early influences in his career.

In an interview with Canadian interviewer and musician Nardwuar, Cudi recalled that his first recording was rapping over music from the influential hip-hop group Wu-Tang Clan in his early teens. "It was really bad," he recalls. "I wasn't that good."[6] He recorded his first demo in 2001, paying for it with money he had earned working at a local restaurant.

Scott spent his first two years of high school at Shaker Heights High School. Then his family moved, and he transferred to Solon High School. It was during this time that Scott began to display aggression and have angry outbursts. It was a pattern that would haunt him even as a successful performer. At Solon, he had several scrapes with the law. The first was an assault charge after joining a fight between schoolmates. Scott said he was an innocent bystander. A second incident involved underage drinking at a high school football game. Eventually, Scott was expelled from Solon for threatening to strike a principal. He ended up later earning his GED.

THE GED

After being expelled from high school, Scott earned the equivalent of a high school diploma by successfully completing his GED, or General Educational Development. The GED is a series of four tests that assess abilities in subjects such as math, science, social studies, and English. Earning a GED allows an individual to access most of the same benefits of earning a conventional high school diploma. Most employers will accept a GED instead of a diploma, as will most colleges and universities, if applicants also have acceptable scores in college readiness exams, such as the SAT or ACT. In order to take the GED, a person must be at least 18 years old and not currently enrolled in high school.

In 2015, Cudi returned to Shaker Heights High School for a TED Talk. He talked about his path from Cleveland to a successful music career, acknowledging both victories and missteps. "I wish I applied myself [in school] as much as I applied all the energy into music as I did," he told the audience of students.[7]

STAND BY ME

Cudi has said that the movie *Stand by Me* spurred him to want to be an actor, a dream that led him to study film at the University of Toledo for one year. The 1986 film, which is based on a Stephen King novella, chronicles the adventures of a group of four boys who decide to seek out the body of another boy who has gone missing. Cudi says he remembers watching the film and thinking, "I want to do that one day."[8] He said he was especially touched by the final scene with actors Wil Wheaton and River Phoenix, and he realized that he wanted to have that kind of an impact on audiences too. Cudi's first acting gig was at age ten when he appeared in a youth production of *You're a Good Man, Charlie Brown*.

NOT HAPPENING IN CLEVELAND

Scott's next stop was the University of Toledo, where he planned to study for a film career. In a Twitter post, Cudi referred to his time at the university as a time when he drank, smoked marijuana, and barely went to class. He was arrested for underage drinking and ended up in handcuffs. While he enjoyed the filmmaking classes, he struggled with the rest of the college experience. "I hated it," he said later. "It wasn't for me."[9] After a year, Scott dropped out of college with a goal of joining the US Navy. However, he was rejected due to his juvenile police record.

Later in his life Cudi would attend a variety of movie premieres, but early on he found that film school wasn't for him.

A move to New York City opened the door to the first big steps in Cudi's musical career.

In 2004, he decided to move to New York City to pursue a career in music. His father's older brother, Kalil Madi, was a jazz drummer there. Madi said Scott could live with him until he got himself established. Scott was quick to take him up on the offer. "I had so many dreams," he

said. "But Ohio wasn't the place for me to execute them."[10] His mother bought him a one-way ticket to New York and saw him off with a tear-filled scene at the airport. "Both of us were boo-hooing," recalls Elsie Mescudi. "We were so hysterical [people] thought I was sending Scott to Iraq."[11]

Chapter THREE

ODD JOBS AND BIG BREAKS

In New York City, the birthplace of hip-hop, Cudi initially lived in the South Bronx with his uncle, the older brother of Cudi's father. He arrived with $500 in cash and a demo tape. As he recalls, the first step was to get a job. "I was walking up and down Broadway dropping off applications everyplace you can imagine from McDonald's to Foot Locker," Cudi told *Music Connection*. It took a few months, but he finally secured employment. "Thank God I found a job because it was enough to get me a Metro card and some studio time."[1] Over the course of several years, he held a number of jobs, including retail positions at Abercrombie & Fitch, American Apparel, and renowned upscale grocery store Dean & DeLuca. "I always had a job," he said. "I was a hustler."[2]

Cudi was working at Abercrombie & Fitch when a coworker introduced him to Dot da Genius, an

Within a few years of moving to New York City, Cudi was becoming a part of the city's hip-hop community.

Dot da Genius, *left*, was a key collaborator early in Cudi's career.

engineering student who made beats. The two began working together at around the same time that Cudi had a falling-out with his uncle. He had to leave his uncle's home, and he didn't have another place to go. Cudi was preparing to return to Cleveland when Dot and his family stepped in and offered him a place to live. The living arrangement made it easier to collaborate, and in 2007 the song "Day 'N' Nite" was born.

By this time, Cudi was becoming a part of Brooklyn's underground rap community. He had posted "Day 'N' Nite" on the social media platform Myspace, where it received decent traffic. It also caught the attention of producer Emile Haynie, who brought Cudi to the studio along with record producer Patrick "Plain Pat" Reynolds. Haynie and Reynolds worked with Cudi to further develop his sound into something Reynolds felt the market would buy. Reynolds also was instrumental in getting Cudi in front of

O's

DOT DA GENIUS

Dot da Genius is a keyboardist, producer, composer, and engineer. He was born Oladipo Omishore on July 17, 1986, in Brooklyn, New York. At age seven his father sent him to the Brooklyn Academy of Music, where he studied piano. He later studied electrical engineering at the Polytechnic Institute of New York University. His professional name came from a combination of going by O. Omishore, providing the "dot," and the fact that he was playing around with beats while studying engineering.

Omishore began programming beats in 2003 and immediately fell in love with the process. His parents helped him set up a makeshift studio in the family basement, and it was there that he taught himself to engineer music. Following the success of "Day 'N' Nite" and *Man on the Moon: The End of Day*, Omishore left the family basement and formed his own label and professional recording studio.

Canadian DJ Alain "A-Trak" Macklovitch, who was aligned with record label Fool's Gold. Cudi signed with Fool's Gold and released "Day 'N' Nite" as a single in February 2008.

At this time, Cudi was processing the death of his uncle, who had passed away in 2007. He felt more pressure than ever to succeed in music. Had it not been for his uncle, he said, he could not have moved to the city. "It was like, 'I have to fulfill this destiny now for sure,'" he told *Complex*. "I wasn't taking no for an answer."[3]

A KID NAMED CUDI

In July 2008, Cudi released his first mixtape,

A Kid Named Cudi. Cudi developed the mixtape with Plain Pat and Emile Haynie. The team dropped the mixtape as a free download in collaboration with Brooklyn-based clothing brand 10.Deep. Crucially, *A Kid Named Cudi* released at a time when the music industry was undergoing significant disruption. The internet had made it possible for artists to release their music directly to fans, bypassing traditional distribution channels. The online release gave Cudi a new way to deliver his unique sound and his groundbreaking, emotion-laden lyrics.

The mixtape featured "Day 'N' Nite," which Cudi

"I didn't have a job for about the first five months there, so I had to make that $500 stretch. . . . My thing to do then was to go to Times Square and just walk around. I wanted to be a New Yorker so bad."[4]

–Kid Cudi

PLAIN PAT AND EMILE

Ten years after *A Kid Named Cudi*, Cudi did a social media shout-out to the people who helped him break out. First was Patrick "Plain Pat" Reynolds, the producer credited with overseeing the mixtape effort and inviting Cudi over for dinner when he knew finances were lean. Cudi also showed the love to Emile Haynie, a music producer of everything from alternative rock and hip-hop to indie and pop. Haynie started out making beats for New York rap legends, including M.O.P. and Ghostface Killah. He met Kanye West at a recording session and ended up working with him on "Runaway." Cudi credits Haynie with helping him identify his sound.

has acknowledged was influenced by the Geto Boys' "Mind Playing Tricks on Me." Other songs included references to pop culture ("Save My Soul"), had Cudi singing off-key ("Whenever"), and featured a variety of unique beats. "50 Ways to Make a Record" sampled singer-songwriter Paul Simon, while "Man on the Moon" introduced a cosmic, spacey sound, which would feature even more in Cudi's future works. For many fans and artists alike, *A Kid Named Cudi* greatly expanded what hip-hop music could be. It also got Cudi noticed by famed hip-hop artist and star-maker Kanye West.

GOING DIGITAL

The late 1990s saw a dramatic change in how the world consumed music. For the first time, music could be purchased in a digital format over the internet. This quickly revolutionized the industry by enabling artists to bypass traditional record companies and distribute digital versions of their music directly to their fans.

Today, services including SoundCloud and ReverbNation are enabling new talent to get exposure as well as promote their work. That does not mean there is no role for record labels, however. New artists still can benefit from access to additional collaborators, coaches, and producers as they refine their sounds, though they may give up some creative control in the process.

KANYE

In an interview, Cudi said he originally met West in 2004 while browsing at a music store in New York. "I was looking at CDs, saw the gleam of a Jesus piece in the right side of my eye, looked up, and it was Kanye West."[5]

By 2004, Kanye West was already a hip-hop star, and Cudi wanted badly to work with him.

Cudi introduced himself as both Scott and Kid Cudi and told West he was an up-and-coming artist. In an especially bold move, he also asked West to sign him to his label. "I had no pitch," Cudi recalls. "I was just this kid that was like, 'Can you sign me?'"[6] West politely declined. Cudi recalls telling West that while Cudi wasn't that good yet, he had the potential to be great.

West and Cudi's next meeting was similarly unplanned. Cudi was working at the trendy fashion retail store BAPE when West came in to shop. "I was helping him get a couple of things," he recalled. "I forgot to take a sensor off of one of the jackets he bought and I had to run out the store to catch him before he left."[7]

BAPE

BAPE, or A Bathing Ape, is a Japanese lifestyle and streetwear brand. The brand is known for its bright colors, playful designs, and collaborations with other brands and characters from popular media. BAPE founder Nigo named the brand based on his love of the 1968 film *Planet of the Apes*.

Cudi learned about the brand when he moved to New York. He said it took several attempts, but he was finally able to get a job at a BAPE store so he could afford to buy its merchandise. In 2009, Cudi teamed up with the company to produce a range of fashion T-shirts incorporating both the BAPE mascot, Baby Milo, and an image of himself.

Their next encounter was strategically planned. Plain Pat, who had managed West previously, sent him a copy of the mixtape *A Kid Named Cudi*. West was impressed enough to show up for the July 2008 mixtape release party. West had been looking for inspiration for his next album, *808s & Heartbreak*. He decided to give the new kid from Cleveland a try. He invited Cudi to go into the studio with him in Hawaii to collaborate on hip-hop legend Jay-Z's album *The Blueprint 3*.

Chapter FOUR

MAN ON THE MOON

Cudi was excited and nervous to be working with one of the biggest names in hip-hop. "When I'm working with 'Ye,' it's always like, 'I hope he likes this,'" Cudi told interviewer Zane Lowe. "It doesn't matter how excited I get, or the people around me in the room get, if he doesn't f— like it, I gotta f— rewrite it."[1] He recalled the time when they first began working together in Hawaii on material for Jay-Z. Cudi said he was anxiously chain-smoking cigarettes on his balcony while working on beats West had given him. After ten minutes, he had one idea that he shared with West. West loved it and insisted they record it immediately.

The beat went on to become part of Jay-Z's "Already Home." For Cudi, however, it simply increased the pressure. "The response was wild in the booth, and I'm like, 'I have to do this a million more times.'"[2]

At the Hawaii recording studio, Cudi finally had a shot to show his hip-hop idols what he could do.

What began as a helping hand on a Jay-Z project quickly morphed into a collaboration on West's next album. Cudi found himself knee-deep in *808s & Heartbreak*. When all was said and done, he had cowritten "Heartless," "Paranoid," "Welcome to Heartbreak," and "RoboCop." Cudi also provided vocals on the album, which became West's most successful release yet. In the fall of 2008, West also signed Cudi to his label, G.O.O.D. Music.

Suddenly, Cudi found himself in a situation in which his dreams were coming true. But the success was coming at a high price. "[The pressure] was nerve-racking," Cudi recalled. "To tell you the truth, it's what drove me to

808s & HEARTBREAK

Kanye West's *808s & Heartbreak* remains a game-changing album in hip-hop. The album's title refers to the Roland TR-808 computer-controlled rhythm machine, a drum machine that provides similar kicks and snares to those used by 1980s rocker Phil Collins, one of West's inspirations. The TR-808 enabled West to move away from the traditional warmth of soul music samples and lyrical raps to an auto-tuned, melody-focused pop sound. "So I'm about to express my stuff with melody. It's a fine line, where you don't know if it's rapping or what it is," West said.[3] The resulting album split audiences, with older rap fans viewing West's latest effort as a disappointment and younger fans getting excited by this new, melody-driven rap that quickly became a popular style.

Cudi's work on *808s & Heartbreak* would be the first of many collaborations with West.

drugs."[4] Cudi said he didn't feel he could go on without the relief drugs gave him.

BUILDING MOMENTUM

Cudi continued working on new music while also gaining increasing recognition for his earlier efforts. In 2009 he was nominated in the best new artist category by the American Music Awards, the BET Awards, and the MTV Video Music Awards. The BET Hip-Hop Awards nominations tapped him for Rookie of the Year, People's Champ, Best Track of the Year for "Day 'N' Nite," and Best Hip-Hop Style.

In February of 2009, Cudi appeared on famed rapper Snoop Dogg's talk show, where he performed "Day 'N' Nite." In April he officially signed to the Universal Motown label, then hit the road that summer with fellow new rapper Asher Roth. Before long, he was back in the studio, hard at work on his next effort, which would be his first full album.

While he admits he could have turned to West for more assistance, Cudi said he was determined to put out something that was more uniquely his sound. He turned to a small group of trusted producers, including Plain Pat, Haynie, Ratatat, and others, to help bring his first studio album to life. "It's important as a new artist to establish your own sound," he said. "You don't ever get that chance again."[5]

For this new album's soundscape, Cudi looked to the past. His inspirations included English progressive rock bands of the 1960s and 1970s, including Pink Floyd and the Electric Light Orchestra. He arranged the album in a series of five dreamlike acts that would introduce fans to his many sides over the course of the songs. The album featured collaborations with West, Common, Snoop Dogg, and several others.

The members of Ratatat had extensive experience composing and performing catchy electronic music.

LADDERING SUCCESSES

Man on the Moon: The End of Day was released in September 2009. It sold more than 100,000 copies the first week and went on to give Cudi three charting hits in "Day 'N' Nite," "Make Her Say," and "Pursuit of Happiness."[6] Cudi also earned Grammy Award nominations for "Day 'N' Nite" and "Make Her Say," which featured Kanye West, Common, and a sample from Lady Gaga. The video for "Pursuit of Happiness" also earned him an MTV Video Music Awards nomination for Best Hip-Hop Video.

It wasn't long before Cudi's musical successes opened the door to realizing another of his lifelong dreams.

Cudi had studied filmmaking at the University of Toledo, yet his musical career had taken priority over his acting dreams. In December 2010, he had a cameo appearance on the drama series *One Tree Hill*. He played himself in several scenes and performed his hit "Erase Me."

SAMPLING

Sampling is when an artist includes an element of a preexisting recording done by a different artist in his or her song. A sample can be virtually anything, including a beat, a melody, a rhythm, or vocals. The sample is then manipulated to make it fit into the new composition. Sampling in hip-hop is credited to producer Marley Marl, who is said to have accidentally discovered the technique when he figured out how to sample a drumbeat from an existing record.

Through his connection to the New York fashion scene, Cudi caught the eye of Ian Edelman. Edelman was the creator and executive producer of a new scripted show on HBO titled *How to Make It in America*. He persuaded Cudi to audition for the show. Edelman said he sensed something special in the rapper, and during the audition he saw it. At one point, Cudi was supposed to say, "Give me a minute." Instead, Edelman recalled, he said something in French, such as "Give me a *minuit*." The producer said, "If anyone else had done it, it would have been a disaster. But coming from him, it was laugh-out-loud funny."[7] Cudi landed the role of best friend of the show's main characters. His character name is Domingo, named after his own brother. Starting in 2010, he appeared in 16 episodes over the show's two-season run and provided many moments of comic relief.

> **"I think he [Cudi] can do whatever he wants."[8]**
> *–Ian Edelman, creator and executive producer,* How to Make It in America

LIFE IN THE SPOTLIGHT

In March 2010, Cudi became a father to daughter Vada Wamwene Mescudi with former girlfriend Jacqueline Munyasya. He said in an interview that becoming a father

Cudi, *second from left,* got his first big acting break on the HBO show *How to Make It in America.*

VADA WAMWENE MESCUDI

Scott Mescudi's only child is daughter Vada Wamwene Mescudi, born March 26, 2010. Cudi broke up with Vada's mother, Jacqueline Munyasya, shortly after she was born, and Vada has spent most of her time with her mother. The couple has undergone several high-profile custody disputes over the years.

While Munyasya prefers to stay out of the spotlight, Cudi has shared pictures and video of his time with Vada at holidays and other special occasions on his social media accounts. In the spring of 2012, he brought her onstage and introduced her to the crowd during a free concert he performed in Cleveland.

was a frightening thing at first. "I just wanted to be a great dad, and I didn't think I was capable," he said.[9]

The stress of being a new father, along with performances, recording, and drug use, all were taking their toll by this time. In June 2010, Cudi was arrested after allegedly tearing the door of a woman's apartment off its hinges. Police found cocaine on him as well. This was not the first time Cudi's anger had landed him in the headlines. In February 2009 he was tasered by police during a scuffle at a private party held in conjunction with the NBA All-Star Game in Phoenix, Arizona. In December 2009, he punched a fan in the face during a concert in Vancouver, Canada. The fan declined to press charges, saying the incident was a misunderstanding.

Cudi's life in the spotlight was also influencing his music. He began work on the second *Man on the Moon* album. Like the first, it told a personal story. "I want my [music] to be like you're reading a novel, not a Dr. Seuss book," Cudi told *Complex*. "The story's deeper, darker, with no holding back."

Part of this darkness was a drug habit. "I started doing cocaine to get through interviews, because people wanted to know a lot about my personal life," he said. "Then I would smoke weed to calm me down—it was the only way I could get through the day without people noticing I was doing it."[10]

"ALL OF THE LIGHTS"

The song "All of the Lights" won Cudi a Grammy Award in 2012 for Best Rap/Sung Collaboration. It appeared on Kanye West's 2010 album *My Beautiful Dark Twisted Fantasy* and featured vocals by Barbadian singer, actress, and businesswoman Rihanna, along with contributions by many others. In addition to Cudi and Rihanna, Alicia Keys, John Legend, Elton John, Fergie, Elly Jackson, Charlie Wilson, Ryan Leslie, and The-Dream contributed to the track.

Rihanna said the song jumped out at her as soon as she heard it. "[Kanye] actually played his album to me . . . and 'All of the Lights,' that was my favorite song. So when he asked me to come up to the studio at 2 o'clock in the morning, I had to, because I loved it, I knew it was *that* song."[11]

Chapter FIVE

MR. RAGER

Cudi has always been open with his fans about his life, including his struggles with drugs and mental health issues. In his second studio album, *Man on the Moon II: The Legend of Mr. Rager*, that transparency plays out as a five-act battle between good and bad. Cudi said Mr. Rager is his own out-of-control dark side. "I wanted this album to be fun, but the dark [stuff] was my life at that time," he said. "I was fighting not to write that."[1]

Man on the Moon II dropped in November 2010 following the successful release of two of its songs as singles. "Erase Me" featured Kanye West and sported a rap rock alternative sound, with Cudi even dressing like rocker Jimi Hendrix in the video. "Mr. Rager" offered a moody examination of thrill seeking as a response to emotional distress. The album debuted at Number 3 on the *Billboard* 200 chart. It sold more than 169,000 copies in the week after its release.[2]

In the second half of 2010, Cudi made some major changes in his life and career. He moved to California and

In 2010 and beyond, Cudi began exploring new creative directions for his music.

JIMI HENDRIX

Jimi Hendrix was an American rock guitarist, songwriter, and singer who rose to popularity during the turbulent 1960s. Hendrix blended rock, soul, jazz, and blues genres and helped redefine electric guitars for a generation. His name routinely appears on lists of the world's top guitar players of all time. Hendrix is perhaps best known for his song "Purple Haze" and for the electric guitar rendition of "The Star-Spangled Banner" that he played at the Woodstock music festival in 1969.

bought a house formerly owned by rapper Fred Durst. He also announced that he was forming a rock band called WZRD with longtime collaborator Dot da Genius.

Cudi also embarked on several new ventures that had spun off his *Man on the Moon II* album. Cudi had collaborated with rapper Cage on the song "Maniac." It was through that collaboration that Cudi met actor Shia LaBeouf, star of the *Transformers* films. LaBeouf ended up directing the videos for Cudi's songs "Maniac" and "Marijuana," as well as a short horror mockumentary also titled *Maniac*. Released in 2011, *Maniac* features Cage and Cudi as French-speaking serial killers. Cudi also collaborated with French clothing brand Surface to Air on a leather jacket collection. The collaboration featured a seven-minute film, *Mr. Rager*, in which he wears one of the jackets.

PRODUCING

Back in the studio, Cudi and Dot da Genius were working on their self-titled *WZRD* album. It included Cudi playing guitar, and it marked the first time Cudi had produced a studio album himself without Plain Pat and Haynie. Cudi made the break with his former team official in early 2011 by announcing that he was no longer working with them and was dissolving the Dream On label the group had created. *WZRD*, an experimental psychedelic rock album, was released in February 2012 and debuted at Number 3 on the *Billboard* 200.

In addition to *WZRD*, Cudi was working on his third studio album. After the weight of *Man on the Moon II*, Cudi said he wanted to show his fans a different side of himself. *Indicud*, which Cudi

REMIXING THE *TRANSFORMERS* TRAILER

As a lifelong movie buff, Cudi frequently blurs the lines between music and film. In 2009, he released a video featuring his "Sky Might Fall" song over the *Transformers: Revenge of the Fallen* trailer. While his song was not a part of the film's soundtrack, the mashed-up trailer created the desired stir in the entertainment business. Cudi says the idea for the project was purely accidental. He happened to be looking at the movie trailer online when "Sky Might Fall" began playing on his computer.

Cudi attended the premiere of *The Hunger Games* in March 2012.

produced, added more up-tempo beats and positive lyrics to Cudi's catalog. The album even included a nod to another of Cudi's favorite movies, Adam Sandler's *Billy Madison*. Featuring collaborations with rapper Kendrick Lamar and indie rocker Father John Misty, *Indicud* released in April 2013. However, it received a lukewarm critical reception, failing to live up to the high expectations set by Cudi's earlier works.

"TELEPORT 2 ME, JAMIE"

The *WZRD* album includes a nod to another personal subject for Kid Cudi. The song "Teleport 2 Me, Jamie" refers to Cudi's then girlfriend, entertainment lawyer Jamie Baratta. The two began dating in 2010 and broke off their relationship in 2012, the same year Cudi and Dot released *WZRD*. In addition to Baratta, Cudi has been romantically linked to actresses Michelle Trachtenberg, Amanda Bynes, and Stella Maeve, as well as Rihanna's stylist Mariel Haenn.

Even as Cudi focused on his own work, he continued to collaborate with other artists in both music and video projects in 2012. He teamed up with fellow Cleveland rapper King Chip to feature in two songs on Chip's *Tell Ya Friends* mixtape. He contributed a song to the soundtrack for the movie *The Hunger Games*. He also starred in a short film directed by Kanye West titled *Cruel Summer*.

ONLY GOOD FOR A HOOK

By 2013, Cudi's relationship with West and G.O.O.D. Music had changed. In April of that year, he announced he had officially left G.O.O.D. and started his own label, Wicked Awesome Records. While he said his relationship with West remained solid, there were indications that this was not quite the truth. The song "Cold Blooded," one of the tracks on *Indicud*, took an open shot at G.O.O.D. and expressed Cudi's frustration about being "only good for a hook, huh?"[3]

Cudi's break from West sent ripples through the hip-hop community. It did not, however, stop his work. In 2013, Cudi appeared in the apocalyptic film *Goodbye World*. That same year, he voiced a character in the animated *The*

CRUEL SUMMER

Cruel Summer is a 25-minute short film directed by Kanye West and starring Kid Cudi. It is the story of a car thief who falls in love with a blind princess. West produced the film in an attempt to surround audiences not only with sound but also with visuals. The project was shot over the course of five days in the Middle Eastern nation of Qatar using three different camera crews. For the film's premiere at the 2012 Cannes Film Festival, West's production company constructed a pyramid-shaped theater with seven screens.

Cleveland Show and played a criminal mastermind in an episode of the popular sitcom *Brooklyn Nine-Nine* opposite Andy Samberg.

"Wicked Awesome is just really, the whole motivation is just bringing authenticity back to the forefront. . . . [Having money, jewelry, cars, women] doesn't determine if you're a real man or not. . . . Wicked Awesome is about being a real human being, making real music, talking about real things that people deal with."[4]

–Kid Cudi

Chapter SIX

HITS AND MISSES

In September 2013, Cudi launched the Cud Life Tour 2013, touring with Big Sean, Logic, and Tyler, the Creator. The Cud Life Tour featured Cudi onstage in an astronaut suit made by Hollywood costume designer Jose Fernandez. Cudi's space suit was designed to remind fans there would be more *Man on the Moon* albums on the way. He teased that he would soon be releasing a new extended play (EP) to tide fans over before the next album.

That EP ended up turning into a full-fledged album, *Satellite Flight: The Journey to Mother Moon. Satellite Flight* dropped digitally in February 2014 with no warning, causing many in the industry to say Cudi had "pulled a Beyoncé." The American singer had done a surprise release of her self-titled album in December 2013. Despite the lack of advance notice, both Beyoncé's and Cudi's albums hit Number 1 on iTunes.

Cudi performed live at the Coachella music festival in early 2014.

Satellite Flight maintained Cudi's tradition of surprising his fans with new twists and turns. For example, the album's ten tracks include four instrumentals. Cudi also noted one other important departure. He told *Complex* that he had given up alcohol while working on the project. "Shortly before tour my doctor discovered that my liver was slightly enlarged from excessive drinking," he said in an interview. "It was another one of those wake-up calls."[1] Cudi said he remained sober during the Cud Life tour as well as during the recording of *Satellite Flight*.

JOSE FERNANDEZ

Kid Cudi traditionally wears a vintage T-shirt and jeans for his concerts. Watching the trailer for the 2013 film *After Earth* gave him another idea. *After Earth* called on the talents of Hollywood costume designer Jose Fernandez. Fernandez, a Mexican American sculptor and designer, has been the creative force behind costumes for blockbusters including *Batman v. Superman* and *Captain America: Civil War*. Fernandez got his start on the set of 1989's *Gremlins*. His otherworldly designs eventually captured the attention not only of Cudi but also of billionaire Elon Musk. Musk hired Fernandez to design the astronaut suits for his company SpaceX.

Building on yet another space-themed album, Cudi collaborated with luxury footwear designer Giuseppe Zanotti to release a futuristic sneaker based on the idea of intergalactic travel. The sneaker was announced in 2014 and would be a part of the designer's 2015 collection.

In addition to the sneaker, Cudi followed up the album launch with a string of high-profile television appearances, including spots on *Chelsea Lately* and *The Arsenio Hall Show*. These appearances allowed him to promote not only *Satellite Flight* but also his role as a pilot in 2014's *Need for Speed*.

BEYONCÉ AND SURPRISE RELEASES

Since the surprise release of Beyoncé's self-titled album in December 2013, the star has released several of her albums in this way. Music industry insiders say this method not only reflects her increasingly low-key nature but also shows she has achieved a level of success at which pre-promotion is unnecessary.

FEATURING SCOTT MESCUDI

Based on the popular video game series, *Need for Speed* starred Aaron Paul, best known from the hit TV show *Breaking Bad*. The film included an original song from Cudi, "Hero," performed with American singer Skylar Grey. Shortly after the film hit theaters, Cudi announced that he had been tapped for an acting role in another feature film, *James White*, and would be curating the soundtrack for that effort as well. These announcements came on top of

Cudi's role in *Need for Speed* was his highest-profile acting job yet.

the news that Cudi would appear in the forthcoming film *Entourage*, based on the HBO series of the same name. In both *James White* and *Entourage*, he was credited as Scott Mescudi.

By this time, Cudi had developed both his musical talent and his comedic acting skills. In 2015, he had a chance to bring them both together on the TV series

Comedy Bang! Bang! Cudi took over as the band leader for the fourth season of the sketch comedy show. "I've always wanted to do sketch comedy since I was a kid," Cudi wrote on Twitter at the end of the season. "So being on the show was another dream come true."[2]

Dreams also were the focus of a major fashion collaboration announced in January 2015. Iconic handbag designer Coach chose Cudi, along with actress Chloë Grace Moretz, to appear in its spring 2015 handbag advertising campaign. The two represented the second installment in Coach's "Dreamers" series, focused on individuals boldly

HIGH FASHION AND HIP-HOP

The roots of luxury fashion brands in hip-hop culture trace back to 1982, when Daniel "Dapper Dan" Day opened a boutique in New York that offered streetwear emblazoned with the logos of luxury fashion brands. Day's collection was popular with customers who appreciated fashion but did not have the money to purchase the authentic items. The luxury brands, however, did not approve of the unauthorized use of their logos and succeeded in shutting down the boutique.

Over time, some luxury brands realized hip-hop audiences presented opportunities for new customers, and they began to work directly with hip-hop performers on designs and specific lines. Run-DMC became the first hip-hop group to get an official endorsement after releasing the song "My Adidas." Today's performers routinely endorse key brands, including Kid Cudi for BAPE, A$AP Rocky for Dior Homme, Pharrell Williams for Chanel, and Travis Scott for Saint Laurent.

Cudi's 2015 release, *Speedin' Bullet 2 Heaven*, was filled with anger and pain.

expressing their own styles as they turned their dreams into reality. Coach creative director Stuart Vevers said Cudi was a natural choice for the ads, which appeared in magazines in March 2015. "Kid Cudi's effortless ease and coolness could not better embody the spirit of the spring '15 men's collection," he said.[3]

Back in the recording studio, Cudi was finding work on his next album to be anything but lighthearted. Through the year, he had released several songs in anticipation of his *Speedin' Bullet 2 Heaven* album. He later said that the journey to that album was an especially painful one. "I just wanted to scream and yell and make angry songs,"

Cudi recalled. "It was the only way I could express what I was feeling at the time."[4]

Complex called *Speedin' Bullet 2 Heaven*, released in December 2015, a 1990s-style grunge/alt-rock album that might be "one of the most polarizing albums of the year."[5] It was the first of Cudi's albums to debut outside the Top 10 on the *Billboard* 200. For some fans, it was a completely different side of Cudi and a blast of creativity. For others, it was messy and uncomfortable. For Cudi, the negative reactions were both a wake-up call and an affirmation. "*Speedin' Bullet* was my last outing as the dark, depressing character that people place me as," he said.[6]

> **"I feel like it's my job to always introduce something new to the world."[7]**
>
> *—Kid Cudi*

ON CAMERA

How to Make It in America had shown the world that Cudi could act as well as rap. He had since turned his on-screen charisma into a low-profile but consistent acting career. He established himself as an ideal casting choice to play the calm, funny, and supportive sidekick. His work alongside Aaron Paul and Rami Malek in *Need for Speed* also had earned him Hollywood's attention. He played a similarly funny and charming character in 2014's *Two Night Stand.*

Two Night Stand director Max Nichols said he knew he needed an actor who could handle a comedic role for the supporting part of Cedric. "Cedric is so funny in all of the scenes that he's in," said Nichols. "He's a character that's designed to steal scenes, and that's what Cudi really does too. He comes in and you can't help but pay attention to him."[8]

Cudi's role in *Two Night Stand* gave him another opportunity to hone his comedic acting skills.

Cudi acted opposite Christopher Abbott in *James White.*

Cudi flexed his acting muscles with a challenging role in 2015's *James White*. The movie is about a young man in New York dealing with his father's death, his mother's illness, and his own personal struggles. Cudi plays the man's best friend, who happens to be gay. "This was way different than anything else I've ever done," Cudi said. "I felt like I had a responsibility to present a different walk

in life from that world." Cudi also scored the film at the request of director Josh Mond, who said he often listens to Cudi's music while writing. "For the score, we asked him to write something that really paralleled the characters and New York," Mond said. "He found something that's really beautiful, anxious, and aggressive."[9]

Chapter SEVEN

MULTICHANNEL SUCCESSES

Cudi returned to the recording studio in 2016 and refocused on his music. In April, he released two singles, "Frequency" and "All In." Reviewers quickly compared the new songs to Cudi's earlier *Man on the Moon* efforts and lauded his return to rapping. The singles ended up on his sixth studio album, *Passion, Pain & Demon Slayin'*, which was released in December 2016. The 19-track effort features collaborations with Travis Scott, Pharrell Williams, André 3000, and Willow Smith.

Passion, Pain & Demon Slayin' marked the return of Patrick "Plain Pat" Reynolds, who helped produce the record alongside Cudi himself, Dot da Genius, and several others. Critics welcomed Reynolds's return and the focus and cohesion it brought to the project. Cudi played a 27-city tour to support the release. It kicked off in September 2017. One notable aspect of this tour was

Cudi's 2016 return to his rapping roots was welcomed by fans and critics.

the role of Virgil Abloh, the founder of high-end streetwear brand Off-White. Abloh designed the tour T-shirts in what would be the first of multiple collaborations with Cudi.

HUMMING

Kid Cudi is known for his humming, starting with "My World" on *Man on the Moon* and continuing throughout his work. According to one expert, Cudi's humming may be part of the reason for his appeal to fans. "When you hum for strangers, it's like opening up and inviting them into your personal space," said professor and author Suk-Jun Kim.

Kim, who has researched and written about the role of humming in society, said he was unfamiliar with Cudi's work before starting his project. Upon reviewing the artist's humming, he said it fits well within his findings. "Cudi's humming is very intimate, because he allows us into himself and shows us his loneliness and anxiety," said Kim.[1]

KIDS SEE GHOSTS

Shortly before the *Passion, Pain & Demon Slayin'* tour, hip-hop circles buzzed with a new rumor. Sources claimed Cudi and Kanye West were in a recording studio in Japan hard at work on a top-secret project. That project turned out to be a new collaborative project, *Kids See Ghosts*.

Cudi and West's *Kids See Ghosts* collaboration put an end to the two stars' high-profile estrangement, which had been more or less ongoing since their falling-out in 2013. Some signs of reconciliation had appeared in early

2016, when Cudi contributed vocals to the song "Father Stretch My Hands, Pt. 1" on West's album *The Life of Pablo*. They shared the stage on both Cudi's *Passion, Pain & Demon Slayin'* tour and West's Saint Pablo tour in 2016 and 2017.

With *Kids See Ghosts*, two of the biggest names in hip-hop were back in the studio together. The two worked on the psychedelic album cover art in Japan with designer Takashi Murakami. They also spent time at West's Jackson Hole, Wyoming, home with the other team members.

Cudi and West released the album *Kids See Ghosts* in June 2018. Critics applauded the collaboration, noting that the two artists' strengths complemented each other while, at the same time, their differences reined in their negative tendencies.

VIRGIL ABLOH

Virgil Abloh is an American designer, DJ, and stylist who caught the industry's attention as the creative director for Kanye West. The son of Ghanaian parents, Abloh grew up in Chicago and earned degrees in civil engineering and architecture before turning his talents to fashion. In 2013, Abloh launched the streetwear brand Off-White, which quickly became a favorite of artists including Rihanna, Jay-Z, Beyoncé, and A$AP Rocky. In 2018, he became the artistic director for menswear at Louis Vuitton. This made him the first Black American to serve as artistic director for a French luxury fashion house.

Cudi and West performed together on an elaborate stage at the 2019 Coachella music festival.

One review noted *Kids See Ghosts* was "the guitar album Cudi has tried and failed at twice; and it's the longest we've heard Kanye speak this year without saying anything awful or otherwise disappointing."[2] *Billboard* put *Kids See Ghosts* on its list of the top albums of 2018.

For Cudi, the project was a much-needed affirmation following several years of struggle. "Working on that record saved me," Cudi told *Complex*. "At the time I didn't know if I was going to continue making music or not, and Kanye was there for me, to help me get up."[3]

Designer Virgil Abloh has been linked with multiple figures from the music world in addition to Cudi, including Kanye West and Rihanna.

> "Months went by, and we just kept working on [*Kids See Ghosts*] and chiseling away at it. It was funny to us when people were talking about how the album was rushed or last-minute. I knew what it took. I was there the whole time."[4]
>
> –*Kid Cudi*

AN EYE FOR DESIGN

The success of *Kids See Ghosts* opened up several design and merchandising opportunities for the always fashion-conscious Cudi. On the heels of the new album, Cudi connected with previous collaborator Virgil Abloh, now artistic director for the Louis Vuitton men's collection. Cudi walked in the Louis Vuitton show during 2018 Paris Fashion Week in June. That fall, he appeared in a *GQ* profile in which he modeled a selection of designer fashions.

In February 2019, Cudi announced his new collaboration with French clothing brand A.P.C. The brand's founder, Jean Touitou, had worked with Kanye West before, but Touitou said hearing *Kids See Ghosts* spurred him to work with Cudi as well. Their INTERACTION #1 collection featured jeans, T-shirts, jackets, and footwear all based on Cudi's understated, classic, minimalist style.

DRESSING LIKE KID CUDI

Kid Cudi's style was capturing attention long before his music made him a hip-hop household name. A photographer for *Complex* snapped Cudi for the magazine's Street Detail section in 2007, and Cudi has been quietly influencing fashion ever since. Fashion-forward fans seeking to copy his style should focus on three key things, according to Canadian men's style consultant Tolu Atkinson.

First is mixing styles. Similarly to how Cudi mixes genres of music, he mixes clothing styles as well, such as combining punk with streetwear. Second, Atkinson notes that Cudi often incorporates vintage pieces into his wardrobe. Finally, Cudi is a fan of styles reminiscent of the 1960s psychedelic fashion worn by people such as Jimi Hendrix.

LOUIS VUITTON

Cudi wore a Louis Vuitton coat to the premiere of HBO's *Westworld* in March 2020.

November 2019 saw Cudi returning to headline the musical lineup at ComplexCon. This time, Cudi had top billing. He opened his set with guests Pusha T, King Chip, and actor Timothée Chalamet. ComplexCon guests also were treated to a view of Kid Cudi merchandise, including items from his collaboration with Cactus Plant Flea Market. His Cudder's Playground booth featured laser tag and a ball pit.

TIMOTHÉE CHALAMET

Timothée Chalamet is a French American actor who starred in the acclaimed film *Call Me by Your Name*. He met Kid Cudi in late 2013 after taking a 12-hour train ride to catch one of Cudi's tour stops. Through a friend of a friend, he was able to secure a backstage pass and had a life-changing meeting with the hip-hop star. "They say don't meet your heroes," Chalamet said of the meeting. "So I thought it was going to be a take a selfie and run kind of thing. And he really inspired me to be an artist in a lot of ways."[5]

ASTROWORLD
THRILL
AND
CHILLS

Chapter EIGHT

SAVING 2020

In early 2020, the COVID-19 pandemic changed many parts of society, including the world of music. Most in-person gatherings, including concerts, were canceled to slow the spread of the virus. Cudi made headlines during the pandemic by launching an app to make it easier for new artists to collaborate and share live performances with fans. Cudi collaborated with producer/director Ian Edelman of *How to Make It in America* to create the Encore app.

Cudi treated hip-hop fans to another long-awaited music collaboration in early 2020 when he and Travis Scott formed The Scotts. They debuted their single "The Scotts" in a special event within the video game *Fortnite* on April 23, 2020. The song went on to become Cudi's first Number 1 single on the *Billboard* Hot 100.

On July 8, Cudi enlisted his daughter, Vada, to tease the drop of another high-profile collaboration via a video on Twitter. "The Adventures of Moon Man & Slim Shady" features Cudi with rapper Eminem. Cudi said he sought

Travis Scott had long looked up to Cudi, so much so that he added the name *Scott* to his stage name.

CUDI'S COLLABORATORS

2020 brought collaborations with one rising star, Travis Scott, and one rap legend, Eminem. Travis Scott is an American rapper, singer, songwriter, and record producer. Born Jacques Bermon Webster II, he adopted the stage name Travis Scott in honor of one of his key influences, Scott Mescudi. A native of Houston, Texas, Scott signed with Kanye West's G.O.O.D. Music and gained fame for his unique musical style incorporating auto-tune—software that alters the pitch of a sound—and a half-rapping, half-singing vocal style.

American rapper, record producer, and actor Eminem remains among the most influential rappers in the history of the genre. Born Marshall Bruce Mathers III in Saint Joseph, Missouri, Eminem grew up in poverty, moving frequently and dropping out of school after failing the ninth grade three times. Despite academic challenges, he loved language and found an outlet for his passion in rapping while still a teenager. Eminem has won 15 Grammy Awards and claims the fastest-selling rap album in history with 2000's *The Marshall Mathers LP*. In 2002, he starred in the semi-autobiographical film *8 Mile.*

the project with Eminem to prove his credibility as a rap artist. He initiated the outreach with Eminem over Twitter, then called on help from mutual contacts to connect directly with the rapper.

WE ARE WHO WE ARE

The year 2020 saw Cudi featured in another HBO series. *We Are Who We Are*, directed by Luca Guadagnino, told the story of the children of several families stationed on an American military base in Italy. Guadagnino contacted the rapper because he had worked with Cudi's friend and superfan Timothée Chalamet in the 2017 film *Call Me by Your Name.*

Legendary rapper Eminem collaborated with Cudi in 2020.

Guadagnino said Cudi appealed to him for the character of US Army officer Richard Poythress because he was not only a talented actor but also a good-looking one. "He just said, 'Oh my God, you're so beautiful,'" Cudi recalled of his Skype meeting with Guadagnino. Originally Cudi thought Chalamet had recommended him for the role, but the actor said he had only played Cudi's music on the *Call Me by Your Name* set and told Guadagnino about Cudi's talents.

Guadagnino says Cudi's character in *We Are Who We Are* is very different from the actor's real-life personality. For Cudi, that was appealing. "It wasn't just this buttoned-up family, nice and neat," he said. "I liked the trouble that's hovering behind them."[1] The eight-episode series premiered on HBO on September 14, 2020.

BILL & TED AGAIN

Cudi continued a busy year of acting in 2020 with appearances in season three of HBO's hit science fiction series *Westworld*, as well as an appearance as himself in the comedy film *Bill & Ted Face the Music*. Cudi, an admitted fan of the *Bill & Ted* franchise since the age of seven, says the collaboration started with a chance meeting in 2013 with Alex Winter, who plays Bill, in Los Angeles. Cudi told Winter he was a huge fan and that if there was going to be another *Bill & Ted* movie, he wanted to be a part of it.

Several years later, Cudi heard the movie was moving forward, so he asked his agent to reach out. Within a matter of weeks, Cudi had a part. "It's a dream come true to be able to be in a *Bill & Ted* movie," Cudi said. "The whole time I was on set, I was freaking out."[2]

Bill & Ted also marked the first release resulting from Cudi's 2019 collaboration with the Adidas footwear company. The company released its Torsion Artillery Hi high-top sneaker in conjunction with the DVD and Blu-ray release of *Bill & Ted Face the Music*. Decades earlier, a Torsion sneaker had been featured in the series' second installment, 1991's *Bill & Ted's Bogus Journey*.

MAN ON THE MOON III AT LAST

In October 2020, Cudi released a teaser video for his seventh studio album. It had been more than a decade since *Man on the Moon* introduced Cudi to millions of fans, and it had been nine years since *Man on the Moon II* introduced his alter ego Mr. Rager. On December 11, 2020,

Cudi fulfilled a longtime dream by appearing in 2020's *Bill & Ted Face the Music*.

Cudi followed up with the long-awaited third album in the series, *Man on the Moon III: The Chosen.*

Man on the Moon III is divided into four acts, and in this instance, the album ends with the final defeat of Mr. Rager. The 18 tracks reflect Cudi's own struggles and successes from the previous ten years. They include collaborations with American singer-songwriter Phoebe Bridgers, the late rapper Pop Smoke, British rapper Skepta, and American

Indie star Phoebe Bridgers collaborated with Cudi on the track "Lovin' Me" from *Man on the Moon III*.

rapper Trippie Redd. *Man on the Moon III* debuted at Number 2 on the *Billboard* 200. The 37-second opening song, "Beautiful Trip," made history as the shortest song ever to chart on the *Billboard* Hot 100.

The album received lukewarm reviews from critics, but the reaction from fans was immediate and ecstatic, with some even saying Cudi's effort had "saved" a tumultuous, pandemic-ridden 2020. In the usual Cudi fashion, it featured humming and pop-culture references, including sampling from films such as *Scott Pilgrim vs. the World* and another Cudi favorite, *Stand by Me*.

Man on the Moon III ends with Cudi's daughter, Vada, whispering "to be continued."[3] Cudi involved his ten-year-old daughter in his work again in late 2020. He continued his relationship with Adidas with the debut of the Vadawam 326, named after his daughter and her birth date.

MAD SOLAR

November 2020 saw big announcements from Cudi the actor. He teamed up with manager Dennis Cummings and producer Karina Manashil to create the Mad Solar production and music management company. Mad Solar went to work on *Entergalactic*, a new animated series for

Cudi has done multiple collaborations with Adidas over the course of his career.

Netflix. *Entergalactic* also marked a new chapter for Cudi, who is the writer and executive producer of the series, as well as its star.

Other Mad Solar projects in the works included a film adaptation of the Brandon Taylor novel *Real Life*.

The book is about an introverted, queer Black scientist making his way through life's challenges in a predominantly white PhD program at a midwestern university. *Real Life* was short-listed for the 2020 Booker Prize, which honors the best English-language novel. Cudi was set to star in the film version.

PRODUCING AND MANAGING

With Mad Solar, Kid Cudi moved into the business side of music and movies. In movies, a producer is involved in identifying projects, selecting scripts, lining up financing, and coordinating writing, directing, and editing. In music, managers work with artists on virtually everything except for the music. This includes identifying projects and advising on performance venues, contracts, and other business matters.

Chapter NINE

A MAN NAMED SCOTT

Man on the Moon III marked a musical milestone for Cudi, and it proved to be a booster rocket for his career. In January 2021, he dropped a remix of one of his earlier successes, a collaboration with EDM sensation David Guetta. The remix of "Memories" came a full ten years after the original single and was inspired by a viral resurgence of the song on the video platform TikTok. Several months later, Cudi also told fans on Twitter that he was working to make his original 2008 mixtape, *A Kid Named Cudi*, available on streaming services for a new generation.

In February, Cudi appeared in the drama/thriller film *Crisis*, starring Gary Oldman and Armie Hammer. In April, he was the musical guest on *Saturday Night Live*. He kicked off his appearance with a musical skit featuring his own superfans Pete Davidson, with whom he collaborated

After more than a decade of success, Cudi looked backward in 2021 to rerelease older material and introduce a new generation of fans to his earlier work.

on the soundtrack for *The King of Staten Island*, and Timothée Chalamet. He performed "Tequila Shots" from *Man on the Moon III* while wearing a green cardigan and performed "Sad People" in a dress.

TIKTOK TIFF

The TikTok platform allows users to set their videos to a variety of sounds, including popular music. The platform encourages sharing videos with memes, challenges, and themes, many of which feature the same sounds. For new artists, this sudden popularity can be very welcome. For more established artists, the use can border on copyright violation.

Kid Cudi spoke out on this topic in 2021. A snippet of "Day 'N' Nite" had become a popular meme on videos, where users featured the line "Now look at this" immediately before showing something odd. Cudi called attention to it on Twitter, saying he was not flattered by the usage. He later explained that for him, his lyrics are important and he wished people would respect that.

Cudi later acknowledged that both wardrobe choices were in honor of Kurt Cobain, once the front man of the influential rock band Nirvana. Cudi has pointed to Cobain, who died by suicide in April 1994, as one of his musical influences. In a tweet after the show, Cudi noted that the dress was designed by Virgil Abloh with Cobain in mind. He also indicated that the dress would be included in a collaborative collection between himself and Abloh's company, Off-White.

BAPE is headquartered in Japan, where the company runs multiple stores.

That fashion announcement came just weeks after Cudi announced a collection with his former employer BAPE. That collection, which represented the largest artist-partnership capsule collection the brand had ever produced, featured 20 unique styles. In fashion,

> **"The thing I love about Cudi is he's unapologetically real. . . . A lot of [your] favorite artists wouldn't be [your] favorite artists if it wasn't for Cudi."[1]**
>
> ***–Price of the hip-hop duo Audio Push***

The fashion world, which had long been an interest for Cudi, started to become a bigger focus of his career in 2021.

a capsule is a collection within a collection, such as a smaller group of clothing items all with a common theme. Cudi also hinted in early 2021 that he was working on his own clothing line, with pieces scheduled to be available later that year.

KURT COBAIN

Kurt Cobain was the lead singer, guitarist, and primary songwriter of the grunge band Nirvana in the 1990s. He struggled with depression and ongoing stomach pain issues, which led to a heroin addiction. He shot and killed himself in April 1994 after sneaking out of a drug treatment center.

Cudi has long expressed his admiration for Cobain and his music, and he even got a tattoo of the artist's portrait in 2020. "I'm obsessed with Kurt Cobain," he wrote on Twitter. "I wish he was still here, so he could teach me guitar tricks."[2]

IN THE WORKS

Cudi made the announcement about a special Kid Cudi clothing line via his Twitter account. He also has teased his fans on Twitter with plans for other future projects, including a podcast, an animated series based on *Kids See Ghosts*, a television series with rapper 50 Cent, more songs with Travis Scott, and the album and show *Entergalactic*. Other sources have

DIOR

reported that Cudi has been tapped to star in an upcoming horror film.

More than once, Cudi has referred to his new ventures as dreams come true. He also says he realizes how fortunate he is to have the life that he does. "I always took it like, 'Oh, I'm some art student that just got some crazy grant to make whatever he wants to make,'" he told interviewer Zane Lowe. "Even to this day, I still feel like that."[3]

TAKASHI MURAKAMI

Kid Cudi and Kanye West dropped a teaser video of their forthcoming animated *Kids See Ghosts* project in June 2020. The two-minute video featured the characters Kanye Bear, voiced by West, and Kid Fox, voiced by Cudi. It was created under the direction of Takashi Murakami.

Murakami is a Japanese artist who has had success in painting and sculpting as well as commercial art ventures, including animated films and fashion. Murakami draws inspiration from a range of sources, including traditional Japanese painting, science fiction, and anime. He is well known for creating cartoon characters, and he also created the artwork for the cover of *Kids See Ghosts*. "We want to see the newest things," he says. "That is because we want to see the future, even if only momentarily."[4]

SOUND FOR A NEW GENERATION

Cudi came on the music scene at a time when hip-hop was experiencing a major shift. Fans began to move away from artists with tough-guy images, instead seeking artists willing to be more emotionally transparent.

Rapper 50 Cent, who was set to collaborate with Cudi in 2021, received a star on the Hollywood Walk of Fame in 2020.

Cudi became one of the most successful artists in this new era because he was willing to be just who he was,

Kid Cudi's diverse and pioneering career has left a distinctive mark on the world of hip-hop.

> "That's Cudi's mission. That's always been Cudi's mission. He's like, 'Yo, I wanna talk to these kids; I wanna let them know they're not alone.'"[5]
>
> *—Dot da Genius*

even through periods of depression, loneliness, and anxiety. His willingness to be himself also empowered and inspired the next generation of hip-hop artists to do the same.

Cudi's longevity in rap and hip-hop, along with his durability and appeal in film, television, and fashion, is unusual in an era when social media can make or break careers in just seconds. Music journalist James Schofield identified Cudi's success as a result of his determination to always be who he is, regardless of where that takes him and his work. "Kid Cudi . . . will never have to force himself to sound like anyone else or anything else," Schofield wrote. "He forces music to sound like him. He defines influence, and influential."[6]

HOW SOCIAL MEDIA HELPED SHAPE HIP-HOP

Kid Cudi is one of many artists who use social media services such as Twitter and Instagram to connect with their fans. While social media is a great way to share news of upcoming projects, albums, and tours, it also can help increase downloads and even ticket sales.

Social media allows artists to reach millions of fans and viewers in seconds. Increasingly, some artists are writing lyrics with social media usage in mind. Kid Cudi collaborator and fellow American rapper 2 Chainz shared in an interview that he had Instagram captions in mind as he penned his *Rap or Go to the League* album. "I can see this [stuff] being quoted," he said. "I can see this [stuff] on somebody's IG."[7] Lil Nas X likewise said he intentionally wrote "Old Town Road" with short, catchy, quotable phrases.

TIMELINE

1984

Kid Cudi is born in Cleveland, Ohio, on January 30.

2004

Cudi drops out of the University of Toledo and moves to New York City to live with his uncle, a jazz drummer.

2007

Cudi records "Day 'N' Nite" with Dot da Genius.

2008

Cudi releases his first mixtape, *A Kid Named Cudi*.

Cudi signs with Kanye West's G.O.O.D. Music label.

2009

In September, Cudi releases his first studio album, *Man on the Moon: The End of Day*.

2010

Cudi appears in the television series *How to Make It in America*.

Vada Wamwene Mescudi, Cudi's daughter, is born on March 26.

In November, Cudi releases *Man on the Moon II: The Legend of Mr. Rager*.

2011

Cudi stars in the short film *Maniac*, directed by Shia LaBeouf.

2012

In February, Cudi and Dot da Genius release *WZRD*.

Cudi wins a Grammy Award for Best Rap/Sung Collaboration for "All of the Lights."

2013

Indicud, Cudi's third studio album, is released in April.

2014

Satellite Flight: The Journey to Mother Moon is released in February.

Cudi appears in the feature film *Need for Speed*.

2015

Cudi's fifth album, *Speedin' Bullet 2 Heaven*, is released in December.

2016

Cudi seeks treatment for depression and suicidal thoughts.

In December, Cudi releases *Passion, Pain & Demon Slayin'.*

2018

In June, Cudi and Kanye West release *Kids See Ghosts*.

2019

Cudi is the musical headliner at ComplexCon in November.

2020

Cudi drops singles with Travis Scott and Eminem.

HBO features Cudi in a major role in the series *We Are Who We Are*.

The long-awaited *Man on the Moon III: The Chosen* album is released in December.

2021

Cudi and fashion store BAPE announce a collaborative collection.

In April, Cudi appears as a musical guest on *Saturday Night Live*.

ESSENTIAL FACTS

FULL NAME

Scott Ramon Seguro Mescudi

DATE OF BIRTH

January 30, 1984

PLACE OF BIRTH

Cleveland, Ohio

PARENTS

Lindberg Styles Mescudi and Elsie Harriet (Banks) Mescudi

EDUCATION

Shaker Heights High School, Solon High School, University of Toledo

CAREER HIGHLIGHTS

Cudi released his first song, "Day 'N' Nite," via Myspace. The song's success led to Cudi's first mixtape, *A Kid Named Cudi*, which he dropped as a free download. The mixtape caught the attention of Kanye West, who signed Cudi. In 2009, Cudi released his first studio album, *Man on the Moon: The End of Day*, which he followed up with *Man on the Moon II: The Legend of Mr. Rager* one year later. At the same time, Cudi embarked on an acting career. He has appeared in feature films, short films, and multiple television series, including *Westworld* and *We Are Who We Are*. As a style icon, Cudi also has launched successful collaborations with apparel and footwear design firms, including BAPE, Adidas, and A.P.C.

ALBUMS

Man on the Moon: The End of Day (2009), *Man on the Moon II: The Legend of Mr. Rager* (2010), *WZRD* (2012), *Indicud* (2013), *Satellite Flight: The Journey to Mother Moon* (2014), *Speedin' Bullet 2 Heaven* (2015), *Passion, Pain & Demon Slayin'* (2016), *Kids See Ghosts* (2018), *Man on the Moon III: The Chosen* (2020)

CONTRIBUTION TO HIP-HOP

Kid Cudi rose to fame during a time of significant change in hip-hop. The digitization of music, coupled with the rise of social media, broadened the genre's appeal and gave artists a more direct connection to fans. Cudi was among the first artists to turn away from the hypermasculinity of traditional rap and instead address raw feelings and emotions in his songs. By openly noting his own struggles, Cudi created new opportunities for other artists to explore wider ranges of emotions in their own works.

CONFLICTS

Cudi has been open with fans and the media about his mental health struggles and challenges with drug and alcohol use. As a teen and early in his career, he had several scrapes with the law due to angry outbursts. Cudi and Kanye West had a public falling-out over West's treatment of Cudi. However, the two reconciled and teamed up in the studio again to release *Kids See Ghosts*.

QUOTE

"I feel like it's my job to always introduce something new to the world."

—*Kid Cudi*

GLOSSARY

APOCALYPTIC

Having to do with the end of the world.

BEAT

The instrumental track of a hip-hop song, typically a pattern created by drums and other repetitive noises.

CATALOG

A listing of related things, such as the collection of songs a particular musical group has created over the course of its career.

CHARISMA

Charm that inspires devotion in others.

CURATE

To carefully select a group of things to present or exhibit.

EXTENDED PLAY (EP)

A musical recording of several songs, longer than a single but shorter than an album.

HOOK

A catchy part of a song (but not necessarily the chorus) that draws in a listener.

KICK

Another term for a drumbeat, which can be electronically modified so that the sound lasts longer.

MIXTAPE

A compilation of unreleased tracks, freestyle rap music, and DJ mixes of songs.

MOCKUMENTARY

A humorous or satirical film created in the style of a normal documentary.

PLATINUM

An award, given by the Recording Industry Association of America (RIAA), that represents huge sales—500,000 albums for gold, one million for platinum, and two million or more for multiplatinum.

PSYCHEDELIC

Influenced by the drug culture of hallucinations and altered perceptions.

SIDEKICK

A person who spends time with or helps another person who is more popular or has more status or power.

VINTAGE

Old but still in good shape and considered stylish.

ADDITIONAL RESOURCES

SELECTED BIBLIOGRAPHY

Hoard, Christian. "Kid Cudi: Hip-Hop's Sensitive Soul." *Rolling Stone*, no. 1087, Sept. 2009, p. 40.

Lowe, Zane. "Kid Cudi Interview." *Apple Podcasts*, 10 Dec. 2020, podcasts.apple.com. Accessed 20 Mar. 2021.

Soeder, John. "Before He Became the Most Buzzed-About Rookie in the Music Business, Kid Cudi Was a Kid from Cleveland with Big Dreams." *Cleveland Plain Dealer*, 27 Mar. 2019, cleveland.com. Accessed 25 Mar. 2021.

FURTHER READINGS

Kallen, Stuart A. *Rap and Hip-Hop*. ReferencePoint Press, 2019.

Klepeis, Alicia Z. *Kanye West: Music Industry Influencer.* Abdo, 2018.

Wheeler, Jill C. *Travis Scott: Lo-Fi Hip-Hop Creator*. Abdo, 2020.

ONLINE RESOURCES

Booklinks

NONFICTION NETWORK

FREE! ONLINE NONFICTION RESOURCES

To learn more about Kid Cudi, please visit **abdobooklinks.com** or scan this QR code. These links are routinely monitored and updated to provide the most current information available.

MORE INFORMATION

For more information on this subject, contact or visit the following organizations:

***COMPLEX* MAGAZINE**

complex.com

Complex is a pop-culture magazine and website that covers music, fashion, and related topics, including extensive coverage of Kid Cudi's career. Cudi has appeared on the cover of the magazine multiple times.

KID CUDI: OFFICIAL WEBSITE

kidcudi.com

Kid Cudi's official website includes links to his music, his videos, and his social media accounts. It also features a shopping section with Cudi-branded clothing.

REPUBLIC RECORDS: WICKED AWESOME RECORDS

republicrecords.com/record-label/republic-records-wicked-awesome-records

The label Kid Cudi founded, Wicked Awesome Records, is a part of Republic Records. The website of Republic Records includes a listing of all the artists signed to the company and its subsidiaries.

SOURCE NOTES

CHAPTER 1. ONE COURAGEOUS VOICE

1. Alex Gale et al. "Kid Cudi Returns, Jesse Williams Gets Serious and Other Amazing Moments from ComplexCon Day 1." *Complex*, 6 Nov. 2016, complex.com. Accessed 25 Mar. 2021.

2. Luchina Fisher. "Kid Cudi Performs for 1st Time Since Rehab." *ABC News*, 7 Nov. 2016, abcnews.go.com. Accessed 21 Mar. 2021.

3. "What Is Depression?" *American Psychiatric Association*, n.d., psychiatry.org. Accessed 25 Mar. 2021.

4. Gale et al., "Kid Cudi Returns."

5. "Hip-Hop: Beyond Beats & Rhymes." *Media Education Foundation*, n.d., mediaed.org. Accessed 20 July 2021.

6. Fisher, "Kid Cudi Performs."

7. Donna-Claire Chesman. "Kid Cudi's 'Pursuit of Happiness' Beat Was Created while He Drove to Ratatat's House." *DJBooth*, 6 Sept. 2018, djbooth.net. Accessed 25 Mar. 2021.

8. Josh Glicksman. "Kid Cudi's 'Man on the Moon' Laid the Foundation for 2010s Hip-Hop." *Billboard*, 13 Sept. 2019, billboard.com. Accessed 21 Mar. 2021.

9. Eric Diep. "They Reminisce: How Kid Cudi Inspired a Generation." *Complex*, 12 Sept. 2019, complex.com. Accessed 21 Mar. 2021.

10. Sean Fennessey. "Kid Cudi: Our 2010 Interview." *Spin*, 15 Sept. 2019, spin.com. Accessed 20 July 2021.

11. Adelle Platon. "Kanye West Makes Peace Offering, Calls Kid Cudi 'Most Influential Artist of the Past 10 Years.'" *Billboard*, 21 Sept. 2016, billboard.com. Accessed 21 Mar. 2021.

12. Jordan Darville. "How Travis Scott Went from Kid Cudi Superfan to Collaborator." *Fader*, 8 Sept. 2016, thefader.com. Accessed 22 Mar. 2021.

13. "'SNL' Cast Member Pete Davidson Says Kid Cudi's Music Saved His Life." *Billboard*, 25 Oct. 2016, billboard.com. Accessed 20 July 2021.

14. "Travis Scott's Collaborator in 'The Scotts' Opens Up." *AceShowbiz*, 14 July 2020, aceshowbiz.com. Accessed 25 Mar. 2021.

CHAPTER 2. THE KID FROM CLEVELAND

1. Sean Fennessey. "Kid Cudi: How He Made It in America." *Spin*, 14 Sept. 2010, spin.com. Accessed 27 Mar. 2021.

2. Christian Hoard. "Kid Cudi: Hip-Hop's Sensitive Soul." *Rolling Stone*, Sept. 2009, rollingstone.com. Accessed 20 July 2021.

3. John Soeder. "Before He Became the Most Buzzed-About Rookie in the Music Business, Kid Cudi Was a Kid from Cleveland with Big Dreams." *Cleveland Plain Dealer*, 27 Mar. 2019, cleveland.com. Accessed 25 Mar. 2021.

4. Soeder, "Before He Became the Most Buzzed-About Rookie."

5. Daniel Siwek. "Q&A with Kid Cudi." *Music Connection*, 4 Nov. 2013, musicconnection.com. Accessed 28 Mar. 2021.

6. Fennessey, "Kid Cudi: How He Made It in America."

7. "Hi, I'm Scott - Scott Mescudi - TEDxSHHS." *YouTube*, uploaded by TEDx Talks, 18 Dec. 2015, youtube.com. Accessed 20 July 2021.

8. Zane Lowe. "Kid Cudi Interview." *Apple Podcasts*, 10 Dec. 2020, podcasts.apple.com. Accessed 20 Mar. 2021.

9. Insanul Ahmed. "25 Things You Didn't Know about Kid Cudi." *Complex*, 17 Apr. 2013, complex.com. Accessed 26 Mar. 2021.

10. Soeder, "Before He Became the Most Buzzed-About Rookie."

11. Soeder, "Before He Became the Most Buzzed-About Rookie."

CHAPTER 3. ODD JOBS AND BIG BREAKS

1. Daniel Siwek. "Q&A with Kid Cudi." *Music Connection*, 4 Nov. 2013, musicconnection.com. Accessed 28 Mar. 2021.

2. "Hi, I'm Scott - Scott Mescudi - TEDxSHHS." *YouTube*, uploaded by TEDx Talks, 18 Dec. 2015, youtube.com. Accessed 20 July 2021.

3. "Kid Cudi Profile." *Complex*, 3 Aug. 2009, complex.com. Accessed 20 July 2021.

4. "Kid Cudi Profile."

5. Joshua Copperman. "Kanye West and Kid Cudi's Complicated History." *Spin*, June 6, 2018, spin.com. Accessed 28 Mar. 2021.

6. Kiana Fitzgerald. "A Timeline of How Kid Cudi and Kanye Became Kids See Ghosts." *Complex*, 8 June 2018, complex.com. Accessed 28 Mar. 2021.

7. "A Bathing Ape x Kid Cudi Interview & Photoshoot." *Hypebeast*, 29 Mar. 2010, hypebeast.com. Accessed 28 Mar. 2021.

CHAPTER 4. *MAN ON THE MOON*

1. Zane Lowe. "Kid Cudi Interview." *Apple Podcasts*, 10 Dec. 2020, podcasts.apple.com. Accessed 20 Mar. 2021.

2. Lowe, "Kid Cudi Interview."

3. Omar Burgess. "Kanye Finally Explains 808s and Heartbreak." *HipHopDX*, 21 Oct. 2008, hiphopdx.com. Accessed 20 July 2021.

4. "A Comprehensive Timeline of Kanye West & Kid Cudi's Rocky Relationship." *YouTube*, uploaded by Genius, 25 Aug. 2017, youtube.com. Accessed 28 Mar. 2021.

5. "How Kid Cudi's 'Man on the Moon' Saved a Generation." *YouTube*, uploaded by Genius, 12 Sept. 2019, youtube.com. Accessed 29 Mar. 2021.

6. Sean Fennessey. "Kid Cudi: Our 2010 Interview." *Spin*, 15 Sept. 2019, spin.com. Accessed 20 July 2021.

7. John Soeder. "Before He Became the Most Buzzed-About Rookie in the Music Business, Kid Cudi Was a Kid from Cleveland with Big Dreams." *Cleveland Plain Dealer*, 27 Mar. 2019, cleveland.com. Accessed 25 Mar. 2021.

8. "Kid Cudi: Mad Man on the Moon." *Complex*, 17 Sept. 2010, complex.com. Accessed 20 July 2021.

9. "Kid Cudi: Mad Man on the Moon."

10. "Kid Cudi: Mad Man on the Moon."

11. "All of the Lights." *Songfacts*, 10 Apr. 2021, songfacts.com. Accessed 20 July 2021.

CHAPTER 5. MR. RAGER

1. "Kid Cudi Explains New 'Moon' Walk." *SOHH*, 20 Sept. 2010, sohh.com. Accessed 20 July 2021.

2. "Kid Cudi's *Man on the Moon II* Sells 169K in First Week." *XXL*, 17 Nov. 2010, xxlmag.com. Accessed 20 July 2021.

3. "A Comprehensive Timeline of Kanye West & Kid Cudi's Rocky Relationship." *YouTube*, uploaded by Genius, 25 Aug. 2017, youtube.com. Accessed 28 Mar. 2021.

4. "Kid Cudi Talks about His New Label and Changing Hip Hop." *YouTube*, uploaded by Power 106, 8 Apr. 2013, youtube.com. Accessed 20 July 2021.

SOURCE NOTES CONTINUED

CHAPTER 6. HITS AND MISSES

1. Joe La Puma. "Kid Cudi Talks 'Satellite Flight,' Sobriety, and His Latest Path in Music." *Complex*, 27 Feb. 2014, complex.com. Accessed 6 Apr. 2021.

2. Josiah Hughes. "Kid Cudi Exits 'Comedy Bang! Bang!'" *Exclaim*, 11 Dec. 2015, exclaim.ca. Accessed 7 Apr. 2021.

3. Joshua Espinoza. "Kid Cudi Stars in Coach's Latest Ad Campaign." *Complex*, 20 Jan. 2015, complex.com. Accessed 17 Apr. 2021.

4. Trace William Cowen. "Kid Cudi Looks Back on Initial Public Reaction to *Speedin' Bullet 2 Heaven*." *Complex*, 8 Nov. 2019, complex.com. Accessed 6 Apr. 2021.

5. Chris Mench. "Review: Kid Cudi's *Speedin' Bullet 2 Heaven* Is Not as Terrible as Everyone Thinks It Is." *Complex*, 7 Dec. 2015, complex.com. Accessed 6 Apr. 2021.

6. Brad Wete. "Kid Cudi Reveals His Struggle with Drugs and Depression." *Billboard*, 22 Apr. 2016, billboard.com. Accessed 10 Apr. 2021.

7. Karizza Sanchez. "Kid Cudi & Nigo." *Complex*, n.d., complex.com. Accessed 20 July 2021.

8. Olivia Niland. "'Two Night Stand' Stars Miles Teller, Kid Cudi Celebrate One Memorable Hollywood Premiere Night." *Hollywood Reporter*, 17 Sept. 2014, hollywoodreporter.com. Accessed 3 Apr. 2021.

9. Alex Gale. "Kid Cudi Dishes on His Deleted Male-on-Male Kissing Scenes in New Film *James White*." *Billboard*, 25 Jan. 2015, billboard.com. Accessed 3 Apr. 2021.

CHAPTER 7. MULTICHANNEL SUCCESSES

1. "A Music Expert Explains Why Everyone Loves Kid Cudi's Hums." *YouTube*, uploaded by Genius, 2 May 2019, youtube.com. Accessed 7 Apr. 2021.

2. Craig Jenkins. "*Kids See Ghosts* Is the Win Kanye and Kid Cudi Badly Needed." *Vulture*, 8 June 2018, vulture.com. Accessed 10 Apr. 2021.

3. Joshua Espinoza. "Kid Cudi Reflects on 'Kids See Ghosts': 'Working on That Record Saved Me.'" *Complex*, 8 Oct. 2020, complex.com. Accessed 20 July 2021.

4. Kristin Corry. "Kid Cudi Says 'Kids See Ghosts' Took a Year and a Half to Make." *Vice*, 19 July 2018, vice.com. Accessed 17 Apr. 2021.

5. "Timothee Chalamet Decided to Pursue Acting Dreams after Meeting Kid Cudi." *Hollywood*, 1 Dec. 2017, hollywood.com. Accessed 20 July 2021.

CHAPTER 8. SAVING 2020

1. Brendan Klinkenberg. "Kid Cudi Wants You to Know He's Happy Now." *Esquire*, 29 Sept. 2020, esquire.com. Accessed 20 July 2021.

2. Grant Hermanns. "CS Interview: Kid Cudi Talks *Bill & Ted Face the Music*." *ComingSoon*, 31 Aug. 2020, comingsoon.net. Accessed 3 Apr. 2021.

3. Chris Murphy. "Kid Cudi Returns to Outer Space; Drops *Man on the Moon III: The Chosen*." *Vulture*, 11 Dec. 2020, vulture.com. Accessed 19 Apr. 2021.

CHAPTER 9. A MAN NAMED SCOTT

1. "Audio Push Speak on Kid Cudi's Twitter Shout Out & Influence." *YouTube*, uploaded by HotNewHipHop, 26 Sept. 2016, youtube.com. Accessed 20 July 2021.

2. Rachael Dowd. "See How Kid Cudi Paid Tribute to Kurt Cobain with His New Tattoo." *Alternative Press*, 25 Aug. 2020, altpress.com. Accessed 7 Apr. 2021.

3. Zane Lowe. "Kid Cudi Interview." *Apple Podcasts*, 10 Dec. 2020, podcasts.apple.com. Accessed 20 Mar. 2021.

4. "Takashi Murakami." *Gagosian*, n.d., gagosian.com. Accessed 20 July 2021.

5. "How Kid Cudi's 'Man on the Moon' Saved a Generation." *YouTube*, uploaded by Genius, 12 Sept. 2019, youtube.com. Accessed 29 Mar. 2021.

6. James Schofield. "Mister Misunderstood: Kid Cudi." *Interns*, 30 Mar. 2016, theinterns.net. Accessed 20 July 2021.

7. "How Social Media Changed Hip-Hop in the 2010s." *XXL*, 29 Dec. 2019, xxlmag.com. Accessed 23 Apr. 2021.

INDEX

ABOUT THE AUTHOR

JILL C. WHEELER

Jill C. Wheeler is the author of more than 300 nonfiction titles for young readers. Her interests include biographies, along with natural and behavioral sciences. She lives in Minneapolis, Minnesota, where she enjoys sailing, riding motorcycles, and reading.